# THOSE SWEE[T] OTHER BEINGS



## Ben's Story: But Is It True?

Agatha Jane

Illustrated by:
A. Victoria Jankiewicz-Pezler

*AuthorHouse™*
*1663 Liberty Drive*
*Bloomington, IN 47403*
*www.authorhouse.com*
*Phone: 1-800-839-8640*



*Published by AuthorHouse 11/27/2012*

*ISBN: 978-1-4772-4693-1 (sc)*
*978-1-4772-4694-8 (e)*



*This book is printed on acid-free paper.*

# THOSE SWEET OTHER BEINGS

## Ben's Story: But Is It True?

Author:
Agatha Jane

Illustrator:
A. Victoria Jankiewicz-Pezler

## 24 December 1995 (Christmas Eve)

From a big hill could be seen a small town at the bottom of a valley. The sky above was covered with millions of sparkling stars and was so clear that they could be easily spotted. The town, as if competing with the night sky, was blinking with the colourful lights of Christmas decorations. The contrast between that huge starry illumination in the sky and the tiny but colourful imitation below, made by human beings, was so strong and exciting that it was hard to stop darting glances between the two. The town was also enriched by a blanket of snow draped over the fields, forests, and houses. All of those elements fitted perfectly, making a beautiful picture and creating a holy atmosphere.

Suddenly, the early evening silence was disturbed by the noise of a moving car. As the vehicle neared the town, the work of a tired engine could be heard more clearly. But analysing the noises coming from the traveling car, it was evident that not only was the engine gravely sick, but the body and other mechanisms of that strange contraption were in a very bad shape, and, as if crying for help, were banging and rattling desperately. As it turned out, it was a ten-seat, yellow school bus.

Just before entering the town, the bus drove by a road sign carrying the crest of a town above its name: *Woodcyplu*. Crossing the town, the bus passed another road sign: *Klukuriku 3 km*. After several minutes it drove out of the forest to a large opening, where on the right side were a number of farm buildings and a medium-sized pond. It was the pond Klukuriku.

The bus drove to the gate of the farm. On top of the gate was a sign, carved in wood: *Ben's Rancho*. The bus passed through the gate and wheeled into a yard, to finally stop in front of the main entrance to an impressive wooden farmhouse. The moment the bus was parked several kids jumped out of it and, with a lot of noise, ran onto a terrace in front of the main door.

Everywhere could be seen Christmas decorations, and on one side of the terrace was standing a three metres-high Christmas tree, adorned with vintage lights and beautifully decorated.

As the children were running towards the door, an old lady came out of the house, helping herself with a cane. As soon as she noticed the children, she dropped the cane, jumped with joy and, smiling, tried to embrace all of the kids at the same time. The whole crowd, with Grannie in the middle, entered the house.

Several people then appeared, mainly women, who helped to take off the coats and jackets of the anxious children.

Everybody was dressed elegantly. Four girls, crowded in front of a large mirror in the hall, were arranging their hairstyles and dresses, making funny grimaces. The most funny was the youngest girl, who was practicing kissing on her hand.

In a big living room, other people were busy making the final touches to the decorating of a huge table, which stood in the middle of the room. In the right corner was a Christmas tree, one even more beautiful than that on the terrace, and in front of the tree was a stack of colourful packages, in many different shapes and sizes. At the base of the main wall was a big fireplace emitting heat and occasionally sparks of burned wood.

The children were greeting the adults. It was very noisy, but in general the atmosphere was a very joyous one. From time to time, outbursts of laughter were heard, caused by funny situations.

A boy entering the salon walked up to a tall, muscular man (probably a sportsman) and greeted him with the typical gesture of a footballer. Both man and boy lifted one of their legs backwards and at the same moment , shouted, 'Freeze!'

Another boy, a six year-old, dressed in the elegant outfit of a marine officer, complete with a cap on his head, walked up to every woman in the room, and then up to each man, and greeted each one of them with a military posture and salute. Doing that, he was very serious, while the all people around were having a lot of fun.

The girls were also very funny. One was walking around the salon dressed in a ball dress, and she greeted everyone with a royal bow. Another, the youngest one, was coming up only to the men and offering her hand to be kissed. Because she was only two years old, while lifting her hand she also lifted her body, standing on tiptoes.

After several minutes, Grannie invited everyone to the table. She walked slowly and carefully, and she took the seat at the very end. When seated well and comfortably, she gave directions to everyone on where they should take their seats.

The children sat near Grannie (seven places) and the adults sat further down the table. When all were seated, it turned out that one place, opposite Grannie, was vacant. Behind the empty chair, hanging down the wall, was a big portrait of an older man. On richly carved golden frame, at the bottom edge, was placed a brass plate with a name: *Ben Cork*.

Following a short prayer, the supper started at full speed. It was evident that, apart from Grannie, everyone was very hungry. Only she was eating slowly, with a kind of graciousness, looking from time to time at her grandchildren.

After several dishes, and when appetites were nearly sated, all apart from the 'sportsman' – who was still swallowing big quantities of food, slowed down the pace of eating, especially the children, who were now playing with their food. The one of the 'spanking' greeting enjoyed himself by 'shooting' beans from his plate in the directions of unaware diners and then pretending that it was not him.

Some of the beans landed on the hair of one of the women. As it turned out those beans decorated the woman's hairdo and made it more attractive than before.

Other children also played making tricks on one another, like smuggling pieces of food from their plates to others. Even the serious 'marine officer' enjoyed himself similarly, dropping a piece of carrot into the coffee mug of the 'sportsman', who drank the coffee lustily, choked, made a strange face, took out from his mouth the piece of carrot and asked loudly, 'Did someone lose this carrot?' Everybody laughed.

Grannie, who normally didn't approve of such behaviour at the dining table, on this occasion didn't interfere. She was rather happy. She looked at the portrait of her late husband, Ben, who had passed away five years ago. The face on the portrait smiled gently and blinked an eye.

Grannie blinked an eye as well. After a while, when Grannie looked once again at the picture of her husband, he sent her a kiss, and she returned it.

This 'exchange of feelings' was noticed by a nine-year-old, Niki. Saying nothing, she observed Grannie and Granddaddy's portrait with attention, but discretely.

At the end of supper, Grannie knocked with her cane and shouted, 'Let's all go for presents!'

All jumped out of their seats, the children first, of course, and they ran towards the hill of presents in front of the Christmas tree. To everyone's surprise, the race was won by the youngest girl, who threw herself on the top of the presents and tried to grab as many as possible of the packages for herself.

The race had its dramatic moments. One of the kids in the race fell down halfway, causing a pile-up. One man lost his balance in front of the pile-up, momentarily threatening to fall into the heap of screaming and laughing children. But after a few balancing movements, exercised with a lightning speed, he stood firmly on his feet and helped to dismantle the pile-up, so the kids could continue the race to the presents.

While presents were being un-packed and the wrapping paper torn apart, it was very noisy again and 'cloudy' with colourful pieces of paper flying about in the air. When all of the presents had found their rightful receivers and been opened, Grannie, who for some time now had been seated quietly in an armchair by the fireplace, knocked her cane. The noise quieted down and she said, 'Please come all of you to me. I have something very important to say!'

When all of the guests had come over to her, she asked the children to sit on the carpet near the fireplace and the adults to seat themselves in the armchairs and chairs dotted around the room. It took some time for everyone to settle. (Some of the children, not wanting to be separated from their presents, brought them along.) Grannie looked nervous, a fact that did not go unnoticed by some of the women.

'Are you feeling all right, Mommy?' asked one of the women.

'Don't you need a pill?' asked another.

But Grannie assured them that she was OK and said, with a voice trembling with emotion, 'Exactly to the day, fifty years ago, on 24 December 1945, something very unusual happened here in this house. And Grandfather Ben asked me to tell you about that on the 50th anniversary of that happening.'

Only then, after those words, was there complete silence. The faces of the children and some of the adults expressed anxiety. Grannie launched into the story..

Having driven his light blue car towards Woodcyplu for many hours, Grandfather Ben was enjoying the views of the region. He was coming to this area for the first time.

A couple of days earlier he had bought a farm near Woodcyplu. As the price was very attractive and because he had dreamed for a long time about moving to the countryside, he had bought it on the spot, without bargaining and without seeing it. The estate agent informed Ben that the house and the accompanying farm buildings would need extensive repairs and renovations, as the farm had not been occupied for fifteen years. He had heard that this region is very attractive. Driving at ease, he admired each valley, each tree, each bird and the picturesque fields and forests.

Approaching the town, he stopped and parked the car in a bay situated on a hill overlooking the town below, at the bottom of the valley. From this site, the town's intricacies were clearly visible, with its own town square (actually an oval shape), surrounded by beautiful, old houses, each in a different style but all with pretty fronts.

There could be seen several small restaurants and shops with fancy decorations. Old-fashioned street lanterns encircled the town's square. A Christmas tree in the middle of the square was surrounded by benches. On that particular evening the town was not sleeping. In the square and in the streets was a lot of movement and activity. People of all ages were walking, and children were playing with snow. Some were throwing snowballs; others were making a huge snowman. People greeted one another, some stopping for a chat. Although the words could not be comprehended because of the distance, a jolly turmoil was heard.

For Ben, who had always lived in a big city, in big-city noise and in a big-city rush, that view was for him shocking, but also beautiful and charming. It assured him that he had made a good purchase. He was sure now that he was entering the life he had dreamed about for so many years. He was convinced that he would now get to live quietly. Standing so, dreamy, he noticed that it was getting dark. He had to do some shopping. He started to drive down the very curvy road to the town.

He was surprised by the friendliness of the town's people who, on seeing him, greeted him by nodding their heads and by smiling or waving. He drove to the town's square and circled it, looking for a grocery. He parked the car in front of one of the shops with a cute name on a name plate: *Abracadabra*.

The shop was very small, with a nice, friendly atmosphere. Several people of different ages were inside, examining and choosing goods. Behind a shop bench sat an enormously sized middle-aged woman who looked like she must be the owner of the shop.

Ben was ending his shopping. The owner realized that she had never seen that young and handsome man before. Starring at him, she asked, 'Mister, are you from here? If so, I would have known you. Are you a tourist? For how long . . . ? I can see that you are not married.' On her coat she had a brooch with a name: *Thruda*.

'My name's Ben Cork. I bought that farm by the pond Klukuriku!' responded Ben, proudly and calmly.

The moment he said that, it became suddenly deadly quiet in the shop; even mice could not be heard. The hairdo of Thruda, normally rich in countless curls, changed shape for a moment, to something resembling a stack of hay. It took more than a second for Mrs Thruda to come back from the shock and continue talking to Ben. Now though it was very carefully, as if she was dealing with someone mentally unbalanced.

Paying the bill and walking towards the door Ben noticed the astonishment on the faces of the other people in the shop. Exiting the shop he managed to say, 'Merry Christmas!'

Ben sat in his Ford and then drove around the square. He saw colourful posters pinned to the trees, inviting the town's people and their guests to attend a feast. The smaller print talked of a carnival procession, Luna Park, and supper with dancing.

Driving out of Woodcyplu and engaging with the main road, he tried to understand the strange behaviour of the people in the shop, contrasting with the friendly behaviour of the people on the streets. What did all of this mean? He still had several kilometres to drive to his new house. He had never lived in a village and wondered how it would be. He lost his way a couple of times but eventually arrived at his new house.

Getting out of the car with relief, he stretched out his arms, took a deep breath of wonderful fresh air, walked around the house and found himself to be very happy with the purchase of the farm and with the prospect of a new healthy life. He decided to enter the house.

Walking straight into the hall, Ben switched on a torch. He noticed some very impressive oak stairs. After a while he turned his head to the left. He heard some whispers and hisses and then noticed also in the moonlight some shadowy figures in the living room. He froze. For a while he nervously considered whether to run away or whether to check what was happening in his house. Curiosity and the fact that he was now the owner flipped the balance. Using the torch he searched out a light switch. He found it, and he turned it on.

He could not believe what he saw. He himself was pale and completely wet from sweat, but more perturbing was that in the room by a huge table was seated a bunch of *different animals*! They were all staring at him.

The table was decorated and bending under the weight of dishes heavily laden with food. In the right corner was standing a poorly decorated Christmas tree, without any lights.

A stylish, large fireplace was decorated with colourful garlands but was without fire. By the table, all the seats were taken, except for one at the end facing the hall. For some time everyone and everything was still and silent. Opposite the empty seat, the chair was occupied by a hen. Next to her, on the left side, were sitting three crows, and further a spider, two mice and a squirrel. On the other side were, in order: three gold fish, a fly, a cat, a dog, and a cock. Between the table and the kitchen door were standing in a row (geese formation), and in strange positions, three ants. They were dressed in housemaid suits and were holding pots with hot, steaming meals.

The garments of all of the diners were unusually elegant and in some cases exotic but nevertheless fitting of the occasion of Christmas Eve.

The hen was dressed up in a blue ball dress, richly embroidered, and she had on her head a crown, made of a carton and matching perfectly in shade with the colour of her dress.

A squirrel wore a nice dress of velour.

Both mice were dressed in elegant jumping suits, each of a different colour.

The spider was presenting himself in his new cosmic suit, which was shining like aluminium foil. Whoever looked in his direction had to close his or her eyes or put on sunglasses to avoid the glare if not actual serious eye damage.

The three crows were dressed in neatly cut suits of the same, beige colour.

The three fish, already gold, dressed also in long golden dresses of tulle.

A dog, a St Bernard, was adorned in a blue and white chequered shirt and overalls.

The cock was in a smoking suit, but with a white top and a pair of black trousers.

The cat was wearing a long tail formal black coat, red trousers, and a violet tie and was sporting a very messy hairdo. He looked like an artist.

A fly was sitting with rollers in her hair and with a pink scarf on her head. She was in a bright, fluorescent dress and was smoking a cigarette.

The first who broke the freeze and the silence was the cock. Getting up from his chair with grace and half-walking, half-dancing, he came towards Ben. He stopped two metres in front of him, gave a royal bow and, bending one leg, made an elegant gesture with his right wing, saying with an English, Oxford accent, 'Sir, whom do I have the honour to introduce?'

'Euh . . . ! Aaagghh . . . ! I am the new owner of this house. My name is Ben Cork,' replied Ben.

'Well, then I am your butler. My name is Albert. Please allow me to introduce the dwellers of this house and our guests on this Christmas Eve supper.'

Pointing at the hen with his wing, in a wide elegant gesture, he announced, 'Our housekeeper and kitchen chief: Bertha.' Bertha blushed in response, flipped her wings and nodded.

Albert continued: 'And now our guests: first, the three crows, who are the representatives of our forest financial stock exchange and the business community.' The crows stood up quickly, all at the same time, nodded and sat down, showing no emotion on their faces.

'On the opposite side are our three lovely fish from the Klukuriku pond.' The fish made shy nods, one after the other.

'And I would like to introduce also the rest of my co-habitants. Squirrel Rudelfin is our singer in the evenings and our housemaid during the day. The two mice, Clo and Flo, take care of our food supply. Spider Bruno fights and destroys dust, and those useless, ugly creatures that live in the dust. Dog Ross is our handyman; he can repair everything – even bad weather. Cat Chopinowicz is our very talented pianist, who played all of Mozart's works when he was just two years old. Fly Buba is the spider's assistant in the battle with the dust. And then, of course, there are the three ants, our waitresses and dancers.'

At that, the ants came alive and made a mini-show with a couple of ballet-like movements while simultaneously holding straight the pots with the meals, not spilling anything.

Ben still stood motionless. Bertha. seeing his embarrassment, came to him and, with a lovely smile, said, 'Dear Mister Ben, your arrival was a very nice surprise for us. As you can see, this place has been waiting for you the whole time.'

Holding his arm she gently led him to the empty seat and with Albert's help sat Ben in the chair. She then straightened up, lifted her head to the highest position and rapidly gave a series of orders to the ants. 'Take back these baked bread with sauce and warm them up. Bring a new set for Mister Ben. Stir the soup, and light the fire.'

After emitting these orders, the head of the hen came back to its normal position. And ants, as ants do, executed those orders quickly and without moaning.

The atmosphere in the room relaxed. Albert and Bertha went back to their places, and the supper started. There was the noise of happy chatter. Everyone was eating whatever he or she wanted, and in his or her personal style.

Ben was surprised and astonished with the taste of the dishes, which were prepared only from vegetables and fruits. There was no chicken, no turkey or for that matter the meat of any animal.

The first dish was hot: fried bread with mushroom sauce. It was followed by lemon soup. The third and final dish was fried rice sprinkled with chopped bananas, raisins and some other fruits that were difficult to recognize.

Ben bent over to the left and asked Albert in a whisper, 'Do we get some meat?' Albert choked and shivered. He burst out, 'How do you dare to eat animals? How would you feel if we were eating you? It is . . . ' Ben quickly interrupted.

'My dear Albert, I was only joking!'

'But please be careful the next time with such jokes,' said Albert, disgusted.

All of the other diners were busy talking and chatting, so no one heard the heated exchange between Ben and Albert. As the diners finished eating, the chatter in the room got noisier and more charged with emotion.

The ants, noticing that all had finished eating, started to clean up the table. The crows were engaged in a very exiting discussion with Bruno on the subject of distribution of forestry products. In an ironic tone, Bruno said that he thought that export was being badly and inefficiently organized. Although he was not an economist, it was obvious from the discussion that he had business instincts. He attacked the crows with simple questions and conclusions, and the crows tried hard to defend themselves using complicated economic terms. 'You, Mr Bruno, you are not right!', said one of the crows. 'We've studied this case for many years.'

'And with what result? You couldn't even manage to export one mushroom!' shouted a now angry Bruno.

Next to them, Bertha, in calm tones, discussed with the three golden fish different diets. Bertha was trying to convince the fish to eliminate from their diets all living worms.

'I, for many years now, have eaten only vegetables, and please look at my figure! I lost half a kilogram!'

The fish were not convinced. They looked at barely shaped hen with embarrassment. But being guests they did not want to hurt Bertha and preferred to nod their approval to Bertha's lecturing than to oppose her.

The dog and the cat were talking about music. 'Dear Maestro,' Ross said to Chopinowicz,' 'can you tell us when there will be your next concert?'

'Tomorrow at 5 p.m.,' replied Chopinowicz proudly.

'And will be performing?' asked Ross.

'Of course me, and our singer Rudelfin.'

'Can I play with you? I can already play the melody of *Catty on a Fence* with two fingers!' boasted Ross.

'What *Catty*? What *Fence*? Are you crazy, Mr Ross?' shouted an angry Chopinowicz.

'It will be a concert of classical music. And that *Catty on a Fence* you can play for those dumb mice, Clo and Flo, who are fans of such songs!'

The mice, Clo and Flo, were all the time gossiping about the meals and about all of those present at the table. They were whispering, and from time to time they laughed.

'It was supposed to be lemon soup? Did you see how that nutty spider dressed up?' said one of the mice. 'And where does he want to fly? On Mars?' The other mouse laughed.

'And what is Bertha yapping about? It's more like she gained ten kilograms! Listen Flo, I saw her one night when she opened a jar full of worms, and swallowed all of them in one go!' There was more laughter.

'This new owner is also a strange guy, saying nothing. Is he mute or what?'

'And look! That redhead gazes all the time at that Mr Cork. And what stupid faces she is doing – flapping her eyebrows. She is probably in love with him.'

In fact, the squirrel Rudelfin was staring at Ben continuously. She tried many times to get Ben's attention, blinking her eyes, but finally gave up with no result, sighing.

After some time, hot herbal tea and raisin cookies were served. Bertha saw that Ben was yawning discretely as he listened to Albert's jokes. Albert, before the climax of each joke, blew with thunderous laughter, so loud that all the diners had to stop their conversations and wait until Albert's laughter had died down before they could carry on. No one paid attention to Albert's jokes any more, as they had all heard them several times before over many years.

To be noticed and heard by Ben, Bertha leaned over the table and shouted, 'Dear Mister Ben, I see that you are very tired! In a while we'll prepare a bedroom for you!'

Next, Bertha ordered Bruno, who had a cigarette in his mouth, and Buba, with a double bottom, to prepare the guest room for Ben. The new owner observed the irritated and moaning Bruno.

'Why is it always *me*? Why is it never someone else? It's always me that has to do all of these dirty jobs. Couldn't that man have arrived on another day? *No*, he had to come after fifteen years. And I am not sure I can still work with that rusty vacuum cleaner.'

Seeing that Bruno was pulling the vacuum cleaner with great effort, Ben wanted to help him, and he gently pushed the little vacuum cleaner, to make it easier. But that help was not appreciated by Bruno, who barked like a vicious dog and even showed his teeth at Ben.

To the confused Ben ran Bertha, who said, 'Do not worry, sir. He always moans and complains when he has to do something.'

After supper Bertha showed Ben to his room.

Grannie interrupted the story at this point and, after a short break, said, 'Well, my dears, it was one of those very rare occasions in the history of humankind when animals spoke with human voices. And on that night those animals were not only talking but were also behaving like human beings.'

All had been listening to Grannie's story in complete silence, and now that she had paused, they started to ask her questions and begged her to continue the tale. Realizing that she would not be allowed to stop at this point, Grannie agreed to continue.

* * *Two days later, just before the end of breakfast, Ben asked all of the tenants to stay in the dining room. Albert stood up, took a teaspoon, knocked it against a big vase on the table, and shouted, 'Silence, please! Silence! Mister Ben wants to say something!'

Almost everybody quietened down, except of course Clo and Flo, who carried on their chatting. Albert bent over the table in their direction and said slowly and with anger, 'It also applies to you two!'

The mice, frightened by this sudden outburst of Albert's, silenced immediately. Albert, still visibly angry, sat down, but he gazed at the mice very coldly.

The short stillness was broken by Ben who, after nodding in the direction of Albert, said, 'My dear friends, as you can see, this house and the whole farm are in very poor shape. I decided, therefore, that in order to live well and comfortably, we have to do a lot of repairs. First of all we have to calculate all of the costs of repairs and make a plan for agriculture production that should provide us with a good living.'

After those words, it became very noisy, with everyone talking at the same time. Ben tried to calm them down. When he realized he would not succeed, he made a sign to Albert, who, as before, knocked a teaspoon against the vase and brought back order. Ben continued: 'For everything to go well and smoothly we have to organize three groups. The first will take care of housework and kitchen. The second group will do all the repairs, and the third one will plan and organize agriculture production. I propose that every one of you in turn expresses himself or herself and declares to which group he or she wants to belong. Let's start from the left side, with Albert.'

Albert straightened up and said proudly, 'I am strong and muscular, and with my sharp beak I can make holes. I will join the repair group!'

Cat Chopinowicz also declared himself to be joining the repair group. He informed everyone that he was very agile and that he could walk with ease on the roof.

The fly Buba said that he would join the housework group.

Ross declared, 'I can lead the repair group because I am more experienced in building and construction work than all the rest of you combined!'

The fish agreed to help in the kitchen work with dish washing,

Bertha appointed herself as leader of the house and kitchen group.

The crows promised to prepare a business plan for agriculture production.

Bruno tried a trick. He did not want to belong to any group, but after the very determined intervention of Bertha, he agreed, resultantly, to continue his dusting operations with the condition that Buba would assist him.

The mice Clo and Flo, having experience in purchasing rations, agreed to organize the supply of building materials needed for the house repair.

Rudelfin and the ants joined the house and kitchen team.

Ben noted on paper the composition of each group and then said, 'I'm very glad that we formed the groups so quickly and efficiently. Please prepare plans for each group, to be ready by 3 p.m. this afternoon. I ask the leaders of the groups to come for that meeting. That means Ross, as leader of the repair group, Bertha, as leader of the house and kitchen group, and the crow Bon, as the boss of the production group. Let's go!'

All jumped out of their seats, split into groups and ran out in different directions following their leaders.

Bertha led her team to the kitchen. Ross with his group went to examine the state of the house. The crows flew out of the window towards the town, to obtain the prices of building materials.

It happened so fast that after about only eight seconds, Ben was left completely alone by the table. He was rather glad to be alone, as he thought it would provide him with some much-needed time and calm for contemplation. He would never have expected his tenants to have had so much energy and enthusiasm. While he was thus left pondering for thirty minutes or maybe an hour, the quiet was suddenly broken by a loud bang made by the kitchen door opening, out of which spilled into the room the members of Bertha's group. First came out the ants, who ran to the table and very quickly cleaned it. The next was Rudelfin who, after she had corrected her dress, went upstairs to the bedrooms. Then followed Bruno and Buba. Bruno, as usual, walked slowly, but when he noticed Ben he increased the speed of his walk and went also upstairs. The last to come out was Bertha, proud and very satisfied. She stood in the kitchen doorway giving the last orders to the three golden fish. 'Be very careful with the sunlight. Use only two drops for five litres of water. Otherwise it will run out before the end of the week.' She noticed Ben and corrected her dress. 'Oh, Mister Ben, you are still here? Maybe you'd like some more coffee?'

'With pleasure, thank you,' replied Ben.

Before his head had returned to its original position, the ants had already put coffee on the table. Bertha, coming to the table, asked, 'Can I join you for a while?'

'But of course; you are welcome any time, Bertha. Please sit down.'

After an exchange of several sentences, Bertha jumped to her favourite subject – the protection of animals being eaten by human beings.

The more she continued her lecture, the more excited she got, giving examples of the cruel treatment of pigs, chickens, and so forth. Ben felt very uncomfortable, and in his thoughts he admitted that she was right. Bertha became very heated and even hysterical, so Ben started to worry about her health.

Dissolution of the unbearable tension came unexpectedly. From the first floor were coming strange sounds. Bertha stopped the lecture, calmed down and, turning her head in different directions, listened with great attention. From above were coming some splashes and hisses and finally someone shouted: 'Vacuum cleaner is on fire!'

'Well, well. That's what I thought. That lousy Bruno didn't change the dust bag again. Excuse me, Mister Ben.'

Bertha stood up and ran up the stairs.

Ben took a deep breath. Thinking about what Bertha had been saying, he became increasingly more sympathetic to her point of view and even thought that he could understand her hysterical behaviour. He, who in general was friendly to ecology and to animals, had never imagined before that he could be, for instance, a cock.

Only now he realized that, if he was a cock or a hen, he would probably behave like Bertha did, and he wouldn't be happy to land on someone's table, burned or stuffed.

He suddenly remembered something from his childhood. He was about twelve years old and he was on a summer holiday. His mother had received a chicken from a village woman. Because his mother couldn't kill the chicken herself, she asked Ben and his brother to do it for her. When they took the chicken from their mother, hastily, and without thinking, they agreed to kill the chicken. They had to cut off the chicken's head.

They thought that killing the chicken would be proof of their manhood. They wanted to show their mother that they were big and strong men and that killing that stupid chicken was no problem for them.

From their house to the shed, where all the tools were stored, like an axe and wooden chunks, was maybe about sixty meters. And something strange happened. Going with that chicken towards the shed their hearts started to melt. The chicken, as if feeling what they wanted to do to it, chirped anxiously, turned its head and looking at them with its sad eyes. By the time they arrived at the shed, the situation had turned around. Neither of them wanted to do that. Following a long discussion they came to a conclusion that they must do it. They too hastily agreed to be executors. They couldn't go back to their mother as sissy boys. They divided the roles. Ben had to hold the chicken and put its head on a wooden chunk, and his brother John had to cut the head with an axe – with one blow, so that the chicken would not suffer too much. Unfortunately the poor chicken's head and neck were cut with several blows.

At first, the beak was cut off, and only with the third blow did John manage to strike at the neck. It was not caused by cruelty, but by the fact that when John was dropping the axe he was turning his head away each time, and Ben, afraid that his fingers would be cut, loosened his grip on the chicken.

From that day, Ben and John did not eat poultry for many years.

Some noise in the house brought Ben back from these recollections. He had some jobs to do, so he finished his coffee and went to his room.

A couple of minutes after 3 p.m., Albert informed Ben that the leaders of the groups were waiting downstairs.

By the table in the dining room were seated Bertha, Ross and Bon. Ben sat in his chair. The first to give a report was Ross. He described all of the repairs to be made and boasted that he and his group could finish all of them, at the latest, within seven days. Ben expressed his doubts that the repairs could be completed so fast, but Ross assured him, saying, 'Seven days is the maximum we will need, but if the weather is good and if the materials are delivered on time, we can finish the job in three days!'

Ben was astonished by these words, shaking his head in disbelief. Ross, seeing Ben's face, got up and announced, 'Mister Ben, don't worry, me and my boys are building experts. Not to waste time we want to start the job at once!'

Ross stood up and went out of the room. Next was Bertha, who in a short speech described her plans and then set a menu with Ben, on which, of course, no meat dishes featured. They also set meal times before Bertha got up and went to the kitchen.

When Ben was left alone with Bon, it became calm and quiet. Bon leaned slightly towards Ben and whispered: 'I like all of them very much, but for short meetings only. I almost fell asleep when Bertha and Ross were talking. I have no interest in what they are doing. By the way, what I have to do with nails and potato peeling and so on, I am born to do business. We have a very interesting business proposal. In our opinion we shouldn't bother with agriculture production. We have an idea for making a lot of money with exports.'

'Bruno was right yesterday – no forest fruits and vegetables are exported. We did some marketing research today and found a very interesting client from a neighbouring country who declared that he will buy everything we can manage to find in our forests.' After a short pause, Bon continued, 'But we have to act very fast because he will buy products from other sources. We propose that tomorrow morning we go to that client. He promised to pay for our goods in advance. So we have no risk, Mister Ben.'

Ben was very excited and decided that, as there was no risk, they would leave early in the morning to meet the client.

After supper, Ben asked Bertha to prepare some sandwiches for a two-day trip.

The next morning at five o'clock, Ben and the crows were already on their feet. Bertha prepared a hot breakfast, after which Ben and the crows departed in a very optimistic mood. Bertha did not get back to bed. She was also very excited about the business idea. She set her mind on loose and imagined that Ben had built a palace and appointed her as a matron of countless servants. The cellars were full of food stored for the winter, and every week there were balls and receptions. Dreaming so, she was doing some work in the kitchen until eight o'clock, and then she woke everyone with a loud singing. 'Good morning, good morning, good morning to you. The birds are all singing so good morning to you!'

All day everyone was on the move. It was all the time extremely noisy. The repair group especially emitted excessive quantities of decibels, as if to accent their importance. From time to time there were heard shouts of pain and moans made by members of the repair brigade. Despite that, work carried on until late evening. They stopped only after Bertha had given her last warning. She told them that if they didn't come down within five minutes she would lock the food in the fridges. After a quick wash, they ran down. Bertha, who had seen a lot in her life, was shocked to see the members of the repair group. They each had bruises, cuts, scratches, and black eyes, as if they were coming back from a terrible fight.

Ross re-assured Bertha. 'It is nothing serious; these are only minor cuts. They'll have disappeared by the time of the wedding,' laughed Ross. 'We have to prove to Mister

Ben that we'll complete the work in three days. Those people from the cities have no idea how to work.'

Bertha looked now at those 'builders' with pride and interest, as if they were heroes returning home victorious from a heavy battle.

It went on like that for four days. Ross had already passed his self-imposed target of three days, but to the last deadline there was still some time remaining. Bertha, however, felt that something was going wrong with the job. She was also getting nervous that Ben and the crows had not yet returned. Ross was rather glad that Ben was not back, as the work was still unfinished. The condition of Ross and his team of 'building experts' was worsening each day; their fingers were so swollen that they could barely hold tools. There was no trace of the enthusiasm and vigour of the first day when they had started the job.

On the fifth day, Albert told Bertha in secret that he was not sure he could continue like he had been doing : Ross had difficulty in hitting the heads of nails with precision, hitting rather Albert, who was holding the nails. Now Bertha realized that those regular, emitted cries were when Ross was striking Albert's fingers. And, as she learned from Albert, the other screams and shouts were being made by Chopinowicz as he fell from the roof of the house. While doing works on the roof, he frequently lost his balance and slid down, landing in the yard, which ended with a big bang and loud screams. In fact, those bangs and screams of Chopinowicz's landings had stopped after three days, when Chopinowicz had placed bales of hay around the house, so he could have softer landings, but the yells while he was sliding down the roof were continuing.

One hour before the end of the seven days' deadline, Ross reported to Bertha that all of the work had been completed. The happiest was Bruno. He couldn't conceal his joy that the dusting job was finally over. He was not so much happy about good work but that he didn't have to work, for some time at least. But the relaxed mood did not hold long, as Bertha reminded everyone during supper that seven days had passed already since Mr Ben and the crows had left for the trip that was supposed to last only two days. All saddened after Bertha's words. Ross proposed to organize a rescue team with the purpose being to find Ben and the crows and bring them back safely. During a stormy debate about the composition of such a search team, Ross interrupted discussions with a loud shout. 'I hear a car! I think that it is Mister Ben's Ford! I recognize the engine!'

Everyone jumped out of their seats and ran with happy cries to the main door. Before they reached the door, it opened slowly. First appeared Ben, followed by the crows, with sour faces. Ben's face was pale, and he looked sad and very tired. All stood in silence and made room for Ben, who went to the dining room and sat in his chair. The crows followed Ben, dragging their feet, and then sat in their seats by the table. All the rest sat down and gazed at Ben and the crows in silence. The quiet was broken by Bertha's voice. 'What happened?'

After a while the crow called Aris, with a trembling voice, started to report about their disastrous trip.

'Total fiasco! Nothing came out of it! Bad luck after bad luck! Just after passing the border we got two flat tyres. During the first two days we were looking for the office of that client. No one knew where he worked or where he lived. We received a new address. As it turned out, he moved from there five years ago. We received another address and then another and at last we found the client this morning, about 1,200 kilometres from here. And the client told us that he retired two years ago and doesn't want to hear about importing our vegetables and fruits. Until now, we have no idea with whom Bon was talking before our departure. He had to be some crook, or some stupid joker, who wanted to play a game with us.'

After those words, Aris, Bon and Athos got excited and red with anger. Aris continued, 'When we get hold of him, he will remember us for a long time! We will make sure we knock out of his head such stupid ideas!'

'Stop it!' interrupted Bruno. 'You better continue to study your books! You have no practical experience. You should first get from the client a confirmation on paper before going on that trip!'

The crows dropped their heads and sat quietly, ashamed. Ross proudly announced, 'Don't worry, Mister Ben. Our group completed the repairs with great success. Today is too dark, but tomorrow you can see by yourself.'

Bertha ordered the ants to serve supper for Ben and the crows.

The next morning, after breakfast, Ben, assisted by all of the members of the repair group, went to examine the house. A very proud Ross showed all the repairs they had made, explaining all the details in professional terms. The presentation was still going on after a couple of hours, and Ben was getting sad and tense. When Ross finished his report, Ben, with shaking voice, burst out, in one long go, 'Who cut the construction beams? They needed a circular saw. Who knocked in the nails? They're upside down. Who cut the planks? They look like they've been cut with a kitchen knife. Who plugged in the holes in the roof? They've been done with toilet paper.'

Some were nearly crying; others tried to defend themselves. Ben eventually calmed down and said, 'Well, well . . . I know you tried your best, but we can't repair this house in such a way. In a day or two this house could collapse. It is very dangerous. I'm sorry, but I must find real building experts.'

Ben asked Thruda for the names and addresses of local masters who could work quickly and cheaply.

First to come was a roof expert. Ben tried to instruct him, but he ignored Ben. He took a wooden plank and two huge stones and, with the help of an assistant, placed the biggest stone under the centre of the plank. On a signal from his boss, the assistant, with great effort, lifted the other stone and dropped it on one end of the plank. This created a lever, which worked perfectly. The boss lifted off with great speed and, in sparrow-like flight, flew over the house and landed on a hay stack. Ben was very surprised by the precision of the flight, but he was also astonished by the archaism of that form of roof examination. The roofer crawled out of the hay stack, cleaned himself of the hay – as much as he could at that moment in time, took out a notebook and, after making some notes in it, said that the job should be started as soon as possible and that it would take him a week.

The next day a plumber arrived. Ben had waited for him on the terrace. The moment he saw a yellow pick-up van, he was sure that it must be the plumber. He ran out to greet him and invited him to the house. They went together to the sitting room where on one side was a round, wooden coffee table. They sat by the table, on which was standing a thermos, a jug of milk, a small bowl sugar and some slices of cake. The first piece of cake the plumber took carefully and shyly, but following it he couldn't control himself and, in a moment, there was no cake left, only some crumbs. To digest such a quantity of food, he drunk at the same time three huge cups of coffee. Then he stood up, stretched his arms lazily, and with no hurry went with Ben to examine the hydraulic installations. The examination didn't last long, leaving Ben deeply worried about the lightning speed with which the plumber could examine the installations, but he decided that the plumber must really be an expert in his field to be able to determine what had to be done in such a short time. When they came back to the sitting room, the plumber was the first to sit by the coffee table. He was a very greedy man, now eating even the crumbs left after the cakes. They drank another cup of coffee, talking about the details of plumbing repairs.

The following day the plumber arrived with some equipment and, to Ben's consternation, with several books about plumbing.

The job of both experts – the roofer and the plumber – was still going on after a few days. The roofer fell from the roof during this time, and he stepped on a rusty nail. The plumber wasn't any better. He couldn't control water explosions from the pipes he was breaking, and while trying to weld he received several electric shocks.

All the time the animals were watching the experts and having a lot of fun, making from time to time ironic remarks about their skills. The best at this were Clo and Flo, who could also be seen falling into hysterics at their own quips.

When Ben found out what kind of experts he had hired, he dismissed both of them and made the decisions to do the repairs himself. The same day he went to town and bought a dozen do-it-yourself books along with what he could determine to be the necessary tools and materials. The most urgent work was finished three days before the feast in the town, so Ben slowed down his work at that point, thinking more about the feast.

On that moony evening, Rudelfin decided to tell Ben her great secret: how she felt about him. Together with Chopinowicz she went to the door of Ben's bedroom. She knocked on the door. 'Please come in!' came out of the room.

Rudelfin went inside, leaving Chopinowicz with a record player in the corridor. Chopinowicz knew that on a signal from Rudelfin, he was to play the record with Ben's favourite melody. Ben was half asleep. Rudelfin, climbing on to Ben's bed, said, 'We must have a serious talk.' Ben's favourite melody started.

He couldn't understand what was going on; he was still sleepy. Rudelfin started to move to the rhythm of the music. She flapped her eyebrow. Her lips neared Ben's face. It was getting hot. Beautiful Rudelfin took off her Canadian hat.

Dancing to the music she took off her tail, which was being held on by a pin, and started to undo her red fur. Suddenly a zip stuck. Ben was confused and embarrassed; he covered his face with his hands. But curiosity was stronger. By gaps between his fingers he was watching that unusual show. Rudelfin, still having trouble with the zip, asked Ben for help.

He tried hard and eventually the zip went down. Rudelfin took off her fur slowly. Ben was shocked when he saw what she had on under her fur. With wide eyes and chin dropped, he saw her bright yellow diving suit. Going out of the room Rudelfin said, 'Well, yes, they told me in the shop that this suit – the latest *Arena* model – would make a great impression. Your admiration is very touching . . . No, no, you don't need to applaud.' Dragging her fur on the floor, she added softly, 'I love you Ben.'—She went out, closing the door behind her.

Ben couldn't believe what had happened. Thinking about this, he couldn't fall asleep for a couple of hours.

The day of the feast arrived. Ben was very eager to go. He felt that he needed a break after weeks of hard work and after so many happenings and adventures.

In the early afternoon, while he was parking his car in the town, he saw someone waving to him. Getting out of the car he recognized Thruda, who was standing nearby with another person. He started to venture towards Thruda. She looked very excited.

'Good afternoon, Mister Corky. How are you? Did you get used to our region? How is the work going on with the house? The plumber and the roofer told me that still a lot of work has to be done. Is that so? Are you alone for this feast?' She looked around.

'Yes,' replied Ben.

He noticed that the girl standing next to Thruda was gazing at him.

'Oh, I'm sorry, I forgot to introduce my daughter, Sophie.'

'My name's Ben Cork,' said Ben.

Turning to Sophie he took her hand and, with a broad smile, demonstrated his healthy white teeth. Both mother and daughter were very happy.

They decided to all go for lunch together in the town. In the square were set tents with benches, stands with beverages and a huge grill on which were burning sausages and hamburgers. There was a camping trolley with chips as well.

After lunch they went to the Luna Park. Sophie was dragging Ben everywhere, even on a merry-go-round, on which they were the only adults.

After the merry-go-round, Sophie wanted a baked apple, and then candyfloss and in the end popcorn.

After Luna Park they went to a cafeteria. Sophie went to order three coffees and three slices of cake. Ben sat with Thruda at a table. Checking to make sure that Sophie was definitely out of earshot, she started a serious talk.

'I see that you like my daughter. She is pretty; well . . . apart from a few freckles. But she is only seventeen. She hasn't had a boyfriend yet. I warn you as a mother, don't hurry with her. There is lot of time; otherwise we will have to make a speedy wedding. She is fragile. Do you understand me?'

'I understand what you mean. But I'm not interested in your daughter. She is much too young for me.'

The word 'few' by which Thruda had described the quantity of freckles on Sophie's face was a great understatement; Sophie's face was crowded with freckles.

They noticed that Sophie and a waitress were coming to the table. They didn't mention anything to Sophie about their conversation. Finishing her coffee, Thruda thanked Ben for the day and went home, leaving Ben alone with Sophie.

Ben and Sophie headed in the direction of a huge tent, from where loud music could be heard. It was so loud that the trousers of one of the men standing near a huge loudspeaker were fluting to the vibrations. People were observing them. From nowhere, one of Sophie's friends appeared with another girl, who did not take any notice of Ben. She was looking around at other people, as if searching for someone.

'From where have you kidnapped this guy?' whispered Sophie's friend.

'From the house by the Klukuriku pond!' answered Sophie.

The girl that came with Sophie's friend, overhearing this conversation, turned around with a jump.

'He bought that farm? You must be joking!'

'I'm not,' said Sophie.

They observed Ben, who all the time was watching the girl who was not Sophie's friend. After a while he turned to Sophie.

'Who is she?'

'My sister!' responded Sophie's friend proudly. 'She's Stephanie – Steffy – Smilk, and I'm Doris. Also Smilk!'

Ben walked over to Stephanie, introduced himself and immediately proposed a dance. Steffy agreed at once. They danced three dances in the style of Fred Astaire and Ginger Rogers. Then Steffy went to dance with other men, who were queuing up to dance with her.

When Ben was standing alone, a little bit disappointed that Steffy had left him, Sophie came over and embraced him.

'Shall we dance?'

'Well . . . OK,' agreed Ben, reluctantly.

He was not fond of the idea, and the dance with Sophie did not go well. To the outsider, it looked as if Ben was trying to move a heavy oak cupboard without legs. To his rescue came Steffy, who appeared with some young fellow with whom Sophie went to dance.

Eventually Ben offered to escort Steffy home, and she accepted. They went via the Luna Park, which was bright with all its colourful illuminations.

After a couple of days Steffy came to help Ben in the garden. It was going very fast. Sophie and Doris came to help as well.

One day Steffy was visited by a female friend from high school. The woman complained and criticized everything all the time. She 'fell in love with Ben', who treated her very coolly.

In mid-February, Ben announced to his house animals that he was planning on giving a big reception. He asked Rudelfin, Clo, Flo and Chopinowicz to look for a music group. Luckily, Woodcyplu was visiting the Great Bear Tysh. The next day Rudelfin and Chopinowicz managed to invite the Great Bear Tysh for a talk with Ben.

The Great Bear Tysh brought a video tape with his best performances. Everyone sat in front of the television set waiting to watch the concert on tape with the famous Bear Tysh.

Ben switched on the projector and inserted the film. On the screen appeared the famous Tysh on a Harley Davidson bike with a scarf on his head and sunglasses perched on his ears. Driving about 260 kilometres per hour, he turned his head to the camera. He was smiling, but his teeth were not quite white, as there were many flies crashing in to them. In the next scenes, in different locations, Tysh was trying to pick-up girls, telling them idiotic stories, which always ended up with Tysh being either slapped in the face or drenched by a beverage. Then, driving his motorbike on a road parallel to the sea shoreline, he noticed a figure of a beautiful girl walking on the beach, in the light of a romantic sunset.

He couldn't believe his luck. He was sure she smiled at him. Looking at her, he lost his balance, drove off the road and straight into a huge pile of rubbish. He came out transformed: On his head was a coffee filter in the shape of a cook's cap; some cabbage decorated his hair; and on his nose was hanging an empty roll of toilet paper.

After showing the film, Tysh was red from embarrassment and apologized for bringing in the wrong film. Ben, however, was impressed.

The following two weeks passed very quickly.

On the day of the reception, a number of guests arrived early, partly to make sure that the party had not been cancelled and partly out of curiosity.

At the hour when the party was to begin, the house was dangerously overloaded. The guests were surprised and some shocked to see the animals. They had heard rumours about them, but they had never actually seen them before. They watched with admiration how the animals performed their work, so professionally.

The house animals were joined by glows, working as Chinese lanterns, and a mole in a dark brown jacket, with very thick glasses, who was boring guests with stories about his scientific discoveries.

The hired music group of the Great Bear Tysh was made up of a duck on the bass, dressed in a black vest that showed her weak muscles; a crocodile who was to play the guitar, with a cigar in his mouth, a violet tie with an orange fish on it running down his chest and a bowler hat on his head; and Rudelfin, Clo and Flo as a choir.

They started to play. After a while some fans started to shout and scream hysterically. The Great Tysh just ran on the stage, dressed in rock style.

His voice was similar to Elvis Presley's, who was still a small boy at that time.

On one side of the room were Steffy, Doris, Sophie, and some of the guests who knew them, and in the other part of the room stood Ben with Steffy's friend, Renata, and the rest of the guests. Renata was telling everyone that she and Ben would get married one day and that she hated the animals and the farm life. She said that she was pressing Ben to sell the farm and go back to city life and his original profession: law practice.

All stopped talking when Tysh started singing a very nice song. He twisted in front of the microphone, singing with such emotion that a few girls fainted. Even the choir were deeply moved, discretely wiping tears off their cheeks.

After the first romantic song, and when the sobbing in the crowd had stopped, Tysh sang his famous rock song, *Baby, Baby.* All started to dance. Even Bertha danced on her twiggy legs, which with no difficulty were lifting her huge body. After five or six songs, with changing moods, Tysh was still full of energy but was wet from sweat. The most tired of all was the choir, which were now groaning not singing.

Tysh, noticing that, proposed a change; he said that Chopinowicz should give a concert on the grand piano. The young people were clearly disappointed at the idea, shouting louder and louder, 'We want Bear Tysh! We want Bear Tysh!'

The situation was saved by Tysh, who jumped on the stage and said loudly, 'Hey! Hey! Folks! Thank you very much for your admiration, but I am not the only artist in this world. I would like to introduce our Maestro, who plays the grand piano, Cat Chopinowicz! Please give him a big hand. He's my friend!'

After that warm introduction, and seeing how Tysh applauded when Chopinowicz came on to the stage, the guests gave him a very warm welcome.

Chopinowicz played and played. The public divided into two groups. One group was listening seriously and attentively, while the other, the rock people, listened for the first few minutes but then gradually sneaked out of the room in search of a bar.

So after an hour of Chopinowicz's performance only about half of the guests were left in the living room, listening to the concert. As Chopinowicz finished, he stood up and thanked them for their patience. He received a loud ovation. Hearing the applause, the rock fans ran back to the living room.

On stage appeared Albert, who announced a half-hour break, after which Bear Tysh was to sing the last three songs.

This was followed by a great rush as everyone tried to get to the bar first. The open buffet was in fact almost empty by this point, however, having been cleaned out by the rock fans during Chopinowicz's concert.

Bertha was prepared for this eventuality, however. She gave a signal to the ants, and they managed to bring out several new dishes of food before the crowd reached the tables. All were admiring the tasty meals and loudly congratulating Bertha. She accepted those congratulations without emotion, as if this was just something she was used.

The second delivery of food was disappearing so fast that Bertha was getting terrified, as she was not prepared for such hungry guests. She wondered if they had eaten for weeks before the party, or if they had just been waiting all that time for the free food. With fifteen minutes left to the end of the break, the tables were practically empty.

The normally malicious mice Clo and Flo, on seeing the situation decided to come to Bertha's rescue. Bertha was by that time almost paralyzed, watching the scene with eyes wide open. The mice ran to Bertha, who was leaning on a chair. They climbed the chair and whispered to her, 'What a hungry crowd! We have an idea! We will ask Tysh to start the concert now. Otherwise these hungry town people will eat dishes, pots and furniture!'

Bertha accepted this and whispered happily, 'Splendid !Splendid! I'll give you half a kilogram of cheese for this. Run to Tysh.'

So off went the mice. Shortly, Tysh jumped on the stage in the empty living room and shouted, 'Hey! Hey! People! Where are you hiding? I can't see you!'

The people in the bar reacted as if they had been struck by lightning. Some dropped their plates and glasses on the floor; all of them rushed at once to the door of the living room. But as everyone ran to the door at the same time, the doorway quickly became blocked. It was getting very dangerous. While people pushed from behind, those in the front, blocked in the doorway, were squeezed, screaming. Tysh, seeing that he needed to avoid a tragedy, ran out of the living room and to the bar by the side door, shouting, 'Hey! Hey! I'm here!!' He disappeared.

This helped to unblock the doorway, as some people ran after Tysh. In a moment, Tysh had appeared on the stage again and people were taking their seats in a rush, but without the previous panic.

Following two very rocky songs, Tysh decided to end his concert with a sad, melancholic song so that the guests would leave the house in peace. It was a good plan, and as Albert announced the end of the concert, everyone went home quietly, in a romantic mood.

In general, the party had been very well organized and had gone off without too many hitches. For many years afterwards those who had taken part in it talked about it and about that strange house by the Klukuriku pond.

One evening, Rudelfin, Clo, and Flo decided to make another surprise for Ben. Just in front of the the door to Ben's bedroom, Clo changed her mind and wanted to leave, but after a lengthy lecture from Rudelfin, she decided to stay. Opening the door slightly, they slipped into the bedroom, and walked on their tiptoes in the direction of Ben's bed.

Ben, who normally was alert in his sleep, heard some whispers and laughing. He counted to three and switched on the light. He saw his guests. By that time he could not do or say anything. They stood in a row and began belly swinging to an Arabic dance, slowly withdrawing to the door. When they reached the door, they ran out of the room, closing the door behind them. Clo and Flo were very happy that they had seen Ben in his bed.

For some time, Ben had been meeting Steffy. One evening in May Ben declared his love and asked Steffy to marry him. And what had to happen, happened.

On the last Sunday of May, in the early afternoon, in a beautiful garden by the pond, the wedding ceremony took place. The weather was very nice. In the bower near the pond was standing: a priest, Ben, Steffy, and two witnesses. Guests were sitting on benches dotted around the lawn. On the pond were swimming two swans, which unnoticed came out of the pond and quietly, without hurry, and in a majestic style, ate almost all of the cold buffet and then chased a couple of children, who ran to hide safely in the house. Satisfied with the lunch and the chase, the swans went back to the pond.

Rudelfin was jealous of Steffy, but immediately after the wedding she met a handsome Brazilian grey squirrel, and she soon stopped loving Ben.

Following their short honeymoon, Ben decided to check his list of jobs that needed to be done. First on the list was the need to organize the farm production. Although he had lived in cities all of his life before, he felt that he possessed a talent for farm work.

First, he bought a horse. It was a very strange horse. Running in the field, on flat terrain, it ran lazily, without enthusiasm, but when there were hills and valleys, it neighed happily, galloped forward, jumped over obstacles and braked rapidly.

On one sunny morning, just after breakfast, almost all of the inhabitants went out to the yard. Ben decided that it was a splendid occasion to demonstrate his riding skills. He put on his brand new riding suit. The long, black boots went on with great difficulty, and a pair of cream-coloured trousers, a black jacket and of course a black riding cap fitted easier. When he stepped out on the terrace, everyone present in the yard shouted with admiration.

Ben, with a dynamic march, made his way to the stable, came out with the horse, fixed the saddle and with an elegant and energetic jump landed straight on the saddle. The audience showed their appreciation with shouts and applauses.

The horse, as if realizing that those applauses were not for him, but for Ben, decided to show his best and earn applause as well. He started with a wild whirling dance. With great speed he performed jumps, sudden braking, sharp turns and other acrobatic numbers. The audience was so excited and loud that everyone still remaining on the house came out. Even Bertha, in a kitchen apron and with a vase spoon in her hand, also ran out on the terrace.

The horse, hearing the increasing ovations, repeated his best manoeuvres, but with greater force and energy than before. He tried also a loop?salto Mortale, but could not complete it, and luckily in the last moment landed safely on his legs. Ben was holding firmly that crazy horse. He tried his best to get out of the courtyard, in the hope that when they were out of sight the horse would stop that idiotic show.

At last, Ben managed to manoeuvre the horse, who rode towards the farm gates. But Ben's hopes did not come true, as everyone ran behind them to the field. The horse seeing that didn't react to Ben's instructions, and instead of going to the forest, turned in the opposite direction and continued his performance near the pond. The crowd performed a half circle and was watching the show from a safe distance. The horse, grateful for all the applause, wanted to end the show in a manner that he thought fitting for a horse.

He galloped at very high speed towards the pond, and just before the bank of the pond broke rapidly, making clouds of dust and deep trenches. Even the best rider could not hold on to a saddle with these conditions. Ben flew off, and after an impressive flight, landed in the middle of the pond with a noisy splash. The horse neighed happily, and all of the others present, as usually happens in such situations, burst out laughing.

After a while, when the surface of the pond had flattened and it was clear that Ben was not coming out, the laughter slowly died out. The faces of the public were showed increasing concern. Even the horse started to run nervously up and down the edge of the pond. In the end, something started to come out of the water. At first, appeared a cap, decorated with white lilacs and weeds. Then slowly came out a muddy black figure. Steffy, who was the most anxious, shouted: 'Is it you, Ben?'

The muddy figure tried to say something, but it managed only to produce several air bubbles. The atmosphere became jolly again. However, when Ben came out ashore, it was obvious that he was very angry. The first to notice that was the horse, who quietly, as if on tiptoes, ran to hide himself in the stable. Others went quickly to their jobs.

In the evening, when things had calmed down and the horse was still hiding in the stable, Bruno and Buba decided to visit the horse. They found him with a sad face, lying in hay.

'You are a great artist!' laughed Bruno. 'And that last breaking was outstanding! Ha! It was wonderful! That Ben was flying like an eagle. And what precision! Aimed right in the middle of the pond! Ha!' Now Bruno and Buba were both laughing.

That happy mood of Bruno and Buba gradually took hold of the horse, who started to laugh also, but not so loud as the other two, as he was afraid that Ben could hear him. When they were tired of laughing, Bruno said: 'I think that Mr Ben will give up riding with you. And if you have so much energy, you should rather dig irrigation trenches. Well . . . it is a good idea.

Think about this. Mr Ben will forgive you everything if you dig an irrigation trench around the house. Well . . . we must go now. Come on, Buba!'

The horse was thrilled with Bruno's idea. He waited until all of the lights were off in the house and then waited another hour, until he was sure that everyone had fell fast asleep. He drew a line half a meter around the house. He calculated that if he dug hard the trench he had in his mind to go around the house would be completed before dawn. After an hour, he had already completed the first part of the trench, about five meters long.

Suddenly, Ross came out of the house, dressed in an old-fashioned sleeping suit, with an oil lamp in his hand. He was sleepy, and he yawned. The night was cool, and Ross was shivering from cold. He noticed the strange heap of sand, and he ventured to the edge of the trench, where he saw the horse, frozen. 'Did you lose your mind? What are you doing there?' asked Ross, terrified.

'I want to make a surprise for Mr Ben. Bruno advised me that if I dig this trench, Mr Ben will forgive me for what I did this morning,' replied the horse.

'Good gracious !What a naïve guy you are! That nasty Bruno made fun of you. Get out of this hole; I'll help you cover it up.'

The horse was almost crying. While he was coming out of the hole, Ross approached the edge of the trench and was struck to see its full size.

'It is incredible. You dug this huge trench alone? It is about three metres deep. Unbelievable!'

Ross bent over the trench, lifted up his oil lamp and shouted: 'What's there? Down in the right corner? Something black!'

'It's probably some box!' replied the horse.

'Before we cover the trench, we must get this box out. Maybe there is some treasure!' said Ross, excitedly.

They started to pull out the box, which actually was a trunk as it turned out. They did it quietly, not wanting to wake anyone, especially Mr Ben.

When they opened the trunk, they screamed with excitement.

'Wow! Gee! Ooh! Man!'

The trunk was full of old, gold coins.

Their screams woke up Ben, who after a while appeared on the terrace with a rifle in his hand. Ben moved slowly and carefully towards the shadowy figures, who were laughing happily.

'Hands up!' shouted Ben.

'It's OK, Mr Ben. Please come over here!' shouted back Ross.

When Ross explained to Ben what had happened, Ben stroke the horse gently and said, 'Well, my friend, you are forgiven for that nasty push from the saddle. This trench will be covered back by Bruno, that wiser!'

Ben was very happy. Those coins found by the horse were very old and brought him a huge fortune. He could now invest in the farming.

The second animal Ben bought was a cow. She was kept in a stable for a long time, so when she was allowed to go out she was so happy that when she ran to the field she danced a part of the ballet *Swan's Lake*. Despite her weight, she exercised pirouettes with such grace that even Chopinowicz, who was an expert in ballet, was clearly moved and excited.

The news of the cow's performance went around the house immediately, and most of the inhabitants watched the cow's dance from the house windows.

After the cow noticed the audience and heard their ovations, she performed the last pirouettes with increased energy. She gave an elegant nod and ran on tiptoes out of the field, back to the stable.

A few hours later, when the cow was grazing in the field, Bertha came to her and started a conversation. 'I would never expect that you could dance so well. You are very talented. Do you know that I also feel I have a talent for ballet? I would like to show to everyone that I can do something besides cooking. Especially, I am eager to be noticed by Albert. If you, the two-ton lady, can make such pirouettes, I for sure can do them as well. Besides, I have nicer legs than you. So please, give me some ballet dancing lessons.'

The cow, who all the time had been calmly chewing the grass, turned her head to Bertha, looked straight into her eyes and answered: 'Thank you, my dear, for your nice words. By the way, I checked my weight recently; I have only 1,600 kg!'

'Oh, I'm sorry. I didn't want to offend you. I meant one ton!' apologized Bertha.

'OK, it's all right. I'll give you the ballet lessons with pleasure.'

Bertha kissed the cow, and in a happy mood danced all the way to the house. She tried to imitate the cow's pirouettes. She was showing some talent.

There was a need for a dog to guard the farm, so Ben bought one. It was a very friendly dog. Instead of chasing out other wild dogs, which were wandering around the farm, it played with them. Ross decided to bring order and to train that foolish dog.

One day, Ross put on his army uniform and, walking in military fashion up and down in front of the dog's house, explained all the rules and duties. The 'normal' dog didn't understand anything that Ross was saying and lay in front of the house, gazing lazily at Ross. When Ross finished his lecture, he stopped and asked, 'Will you remember all these rules?'

The dog put his head on his leg and yawned. Ross repeated his lecture about three times, but the dog, seeing that Ross was getting angry, went back to his house and watched Ross from the inside. The dog was clearly not interested in what Ross was saying and demonstrated this with louder and longer yawns. Eventually, Ross gave up and went home.

After two weeks the dog disappeared. Someone spotted a spaniel before the escape, visiting the dog, and it was believed that it probably helped the dog in the escape.

Some months later, the dog returned. But it was not alone. It brought its whole family: his wife, the spaniel, and six very cute puppies.

Everyone was happy. Even Ross welcomed the dog and its family with a military salute.

Ben purchased a goat and five more cows.

One morning he took a stool and a big bucket and went to milk the goat. He sat by the goat and started to milk it. The goat was very embarrassed and couldn't stand it any more. It jumped and kicked Ben straight in the eye. It instantly went black. Ben was very angry. He got hold of the goat by the horns and dragged it into the stable.

Steffy and the others saw the events through the windows. They were worried. Steffy decided to go to the stable. Entering it, she heard the voice of Ben, but she couldn't see him. She went further, until she saw something incredible. Between the enormous cows was that little goat, connected to a milking machine. The goat looked at Steffy with a sad face. He was clearly very frightened.

In the evening, after supper, Rudelfin went to see the goat, who she found crying. Rudelfin kneeled to feed the goat and, doing so, talked to him. 'You know that Mr Ben didn't want to harm you. That kick in the eye wasn't a good idea. Now eat something. Tomorrow is another day, and you will forget about that, and everything will be all right.'

The goat looked up at Rudelfin, and as if understanding, nodded its head. When the goat had finished all the food, Rudelfin got up, saying, 'Bye, bye, you little karate master!' She ran home.

Ben promised his wife that in the spring he would buy some chickens and a cock. During the winter, Steffy saw Ben very rarely. For whole days and evenings Ben was building something in the shed near the stable, and he didn't allow anybody to see what he was doing.

At last spring came.

One day Ben invited everybody to his workshop. Steffy thought that Ben had bought her a new car. She dreamed of having a Ford Cabriolet. But when Ben pulled off a cover from the huge thing standing in the middle of the workshop, it turned out to be something very different

Nevertheless, it was a big surprise. All were astonished. What they saw was really exceptional, not to be seen anywhere on earth.

It was a chicken house. It was not a normal one, however; it was a palace. There were two storeys with pillars in a light blue colour. The rest of the building was pink. The next morning the palace was moved out of the workshop and placed near the pond. In the afternoon, Ben brought home from town twenty hens and one cock. The most excited and curious was Albert, who while greeting new arrivals fell in love at first sight with one of the hens. That same evening Albert invited the cock to the bar, for blackberry juice and a chat.

Albert didn't know how to get to the point, and the conversation was dull and stiff, but after the first blackberry juice he became more bold and went ahead. 'You know that you and me are cousins. You're a cock and I'm a cock. So I'll tell you straight away. That girl Kikiru, I like her very much. Would you introduce us?'

Albert put his wing on the cock's shoulder. The cock turned to Albert nervously. 'Well, you must know, Albert, I like her, too.'

'But you have so many to choose from. I can't live without her. I love her.' He whispered the last words from emotion.

'OK, OK. If you are so serious, I'll help you.'

The next day, Albert went to Bertha to ask her to prepare tasty meals. Bertha tried everything to force Albert to cancel that supper. She made some very malicious and nasty remarks about Kikiru.

'Albert, my love, she is useless; she can't do anything. And she has no figure!'Pulling in her belly, she added, 'She has no waist!'

Swinging slightly, she tried to demonstrate her figure. Albert didn't take any notice of the show. 'I'm in love with her. She is so . . . ' started Albert.

'I thought you loved me!' interrupted Bertha.

Albert, half dreaming, did not hear clearly and asked, 'What did you say?'

Bertha, disappointed and saddened, replied, 'Well, I'll prepare the supper. So, tomorrow, what time?'

'Eight o'clock. In the summer house – by the pond. There has to be candles, blue serviettes and fresh water from the well. There should be a little bit of grain, some carrots and of course corn. I'll ask Chopinowicz to organize some romantic music.'

Albert left a depressed Bertha in the kitchen and ran to the chicken palace to invite Kikiru for the supper.

When Albert left, poor Bertha started to cry, but when she heard some steps, she wiped off her tears and calmed down. The ants entered the kitchen, and she informed them about the supper. Thinking about everything, she decided not to give up but rather to fight for Albert's love.

The next evening, at a quarter to eight, Albert was already waiting in the bower, walking nervously around the beautifully decorated table, laid out for two. In the middle of the table stood a vase, holding a single red rose, and two lanterns.

Albert was always elegant, but now he was at his very best. He was in a black, long tailcoat, a violet tie, and a pair of brand new shoes that he had bought especially for the occasion.

Exactly at eight, Kikiru appeared, dressed in a long, blue evening dress. Albert had the impression that he had seen that dress before, but he wasn't sure when or on whom. He was so excited to see Kikiru anyway that he quickly forgot about everything else and started to entertain his love one. He jumped forward, pulled out a chair and helped Kikiru to sit down. He then sat on his own chair and, leaning slightly over the table, lit the lanterns. He whispered gently, 'You look beautiful! What a pretty dress. But your eyes are the most beautiful on this globe!'

Having heard such such chatter many times before, Kikiru was unimpressed.

'As for the dress, Bertha lent it to me. And I know I have nice eyes. Where did you get these stinking, ever-burning fires from – a cemetery?'

Albert, a little bit surprised and somewhat ashamed, responded, 'Oh, I couldn't find any candles, so I borrowed these ever-burning fires. You are right, they really stink!'

'They poison the air! Look at this poor rose!' Kikiru continued her attack.

In fact, the rose had lost almost all of its petals; only one was left, shivering, as if trying desperately to hold on. Albert jumped out of the chair, moved the ever-burning fires to another table and extinguished them.

To repair the damage, he proposed a toast for their happiness. He filled two crystal glasses with tomato juice and gave one of them to Kikiru. She stood up, reluctantly, but getting less angry, and she struck her glass against Albert's. They both lifted their glasses to their mouths. Before Albert could even taste his drink, Kikiru had drunk hers. *She must have been very thirsty*, thought Albert.

To his horror, Kikiru suddenly choked, went purple, coughed and released a fountain of the tomato juice in Albert's direction. Albert found himself covered from the waist up in loads of red spots. He stood, motionless. Kikiru put her glass on the table and yelled with anger. 'What a stupid joke! You wanted to poison me?'

Albert was still in shock, but he managed to utter, 'What's this? What happened?'

'Try it! You jerk!'

Albert lifted his glass, which he had been holding the whole time, and he tasted the juice. He grimaced. 'What rubbish! Bertha gave me this!'

It took some time for Albert to calm Kikiru down and convince her to stay. He served her a glass of nice, cold water, which improved the mood between them, and soon the atmosphere was getting romantic.

When Kikiru heard some strange noises, she looked under the table, as if she sensed that something was hiding there. Albert realized that it was his stomach that was making screeching noises. He crowed, and after a while the ants came, serving some brightly coloured dishes that proved to be very tasty. Again everything was nice and blissful.

On a signal from Albert, the ants quickly cleaned the table. When the ants had disappeared, from nowhere came some dance music. Kikiru was now relaxed and even nice. Albert got up, made an elegant bow and asked her for a dance. When they were swinging around the bower, Kikiru had to push out Albert several times, as he was dancing far too close to her.

Suddenly, Albert noticed that his loved one was only in her underwear. He looked down and saw Kikiru's dress lying on the floor. Kikiru was so moody that she didn't notice that.

They danced and danced, and Albert was searching desperately in his mind for ideas of how to get out of this situation, but his face was smiling and not showing any of the torment that was going on in his head. He behaved like before, trying to hug her and whisper compliments.

He knew he first had to remove the dress, which was being squashed under her feet. He moved several steps to one side and with an expertly executed kick removed the dress from the floor. It landed in the bush, out of sight. They kept dancing.

Albert, holding his smiling face, was still thinking hard about what to do when Kikiru inevitably found out that she was left in underwear. But after a while he decided to stop thinking about this and have a nice time instead.

*Somehow, everything will come all right,* he thought. But danger came unexpectedly. After a short burst of very cold wind, Kikiru started to shiver slightly. Kikiru stopped the dance and whispered, 'It's getting cold. Let's go home.' Albert felt sad.

Albert quickly took his coat off and put it on her shoulders. That stalled Kikiru for some minutes. Then she complained that her knees were cold. Albert decided not to overdo it and that it would be better to escort her back home.

It was dark by this point, and Albert wondered whether she would notice that she had lost her dress. He was glad that he had dressed for the supper in the long tailcoat, which was now almost completely covering Kikiru's body.

'You are right, my dear, it is getting really cold. Please allow me to escort you home,' he said loudly.

When they reached the door of the 'palace', she kissed him, saying, 'Thank you very much for such a lovely evening, Albert.'

'Goodnight, darling.'

After exchanging kisses in the air, each went back to their own home.

Only some months after Albert's and Kikiru's wedding did Bertha admit to all of the nasty things she had planned and executed that night. She had added some used motor oil to the ever-burning fires. To the tomato juice she had added three spoons of pepper. The dress she had re-made in such a way that it had to get loose because the hangers were sewn in by single threads. She apologized for all those dirty tricks, and she wished them a happy marriage with lots of chicks.

Autumn came. The first eggs appeared in the chicken palace, so Ben decided to go and fetch some. Some of the inhabitants asked him not to go; some volunteered to go in his place. They all told him that it was a very dangerous activity, as chickens hated it when someone tried to pinch their eggs, and they were likely to attack intruders. But Ben didn't listen, and he went alone.

He dressed in layers for the occasion, along with a pair of long fishing boots, heavy-duty gloves, a blue shawl to cover his neck and part of his face, and sunglasses to protect his eyes. And of course he wore a helmet to protect his head.

While Ben was marching to the chicken place, all were nervous, watching the scene. The girls were biting their fingernails, and the boys followed Ben at a safe distance, just in case their help would be needed. Before entering the palace, Ben stopped for a second and waved. He then walked in. What followed next is very difficult to describe.

To the outsiders, something terrible was happening inside the palace. The roof was jumping up and down, the walls were bending and screams could be heard.

After about five minutes, Ben came out of the palace. His clothes were covered in feathers. On his helmet was sitting a cock, singing triumphantly. 'Kukurikuuuuu!'

Everyone ran to the yard, to Ben, who tried to smile. He had put so much effort into collecting the eggs that when he saw that he had only managed to collect a couple of them, he fainted.

Bertha jumped on Ben's belly, listing loudly and clearly all of the animal protection laws. When Ben regained conscience, he managed to say with a shaky voice, 'There are ostriches in there! They were the ones who kicked me so badly. No one is allowed to go in there. They are very aggressive. They don't want to give up the eggs!'

Bertha, seeing the state of Ben, decided to calm the situation down, saying, 'That's right. These ostriches went too far with that kicking. But no wonder, as they were defending their children. I beg you Mr Ben that you don't do it again.'

Some of the boys lifted Ben up, brought him home and put him in bed.

Despite those first disasters, the farming got better with time, and whenever monotony started to take hold, something always happened that would excite again all of the living creatures on the farm. One of the best moments was when Steffy announced that she was expecting a baby. Ben was very happy and prepared a very nice room for the baby.

One evening, Steffy felt some pain. A doctor and nurse were called. They came very fast. They entered the house with a big blast. The nurse was the bass player of the band that had performed at the concert; the doctor was the mole, who had also been at the concert. Everyone was in the hall, and the nurse was pushing herself through the crowd, coming towards Ben, who showed her the way to Steffy's room. First the doctor went to Steffy. The nurse was calming down the hysterical inhabitants. After that she went to Steffy as well. All faces were sad and frightened.

Suddenly, the nurse jumped out of the room, asking for some water. Steffy's cries stopped. Some in the crowd were sobbing quietly, but with time all except Ben fell asleep. Almost at dawn, the stillness, only interrupted by the occasional snoring of Ross, was broken by the sudden cry of a baby. All jumped on their feet. First came out the doctor, who looked terribly tired. Saying nothing she went to a sofa, laid down, and fell into a very deep sleep. After half an hour the nurse came out with a big smile, giving the wrapped baby to Ben. Everyone shouted happily and congratulated Ben. And the Great Bear Tysh flew from Los Angeles, where he had been notified about the arrival of the baby, and he started to sing his famous lullaby song. 'Luu . . . Luu . . . Luu . . . La . . . Lally . . . Du . . . '

'You probably know by now that Steffy was me. But most strange in this story was that those animals not only spoke on Christmas Eve in 1945, but they behaved and worked like human beings for many years after that. However, the fates of these animals took different turns . . .

'The ants joined an ice-skating dancing group and also took part in several television commercials. Recently, I saw them in a Volkswagen commercial for the newest Polo model.

'The fate of the three golden fish took rather a dramatic turn. Around 1952 a sheik from Kuwait arrived with his court in Woodcyplu for a hunting tour. During his sightseeing of the countryside, he "found" in the Klukuriku pond our three dear golden fish, and he kidnapped them and took them back with him to Kuwait. When we demanded that he bring them back, he replied that he would let them go only after nine wishes – three for each fish – were fulfilled.

'In fact, they had very good living conditions in Kuwait. They were well fed, and they lived in a nice, big aquarium. However, we wanted them back. After fulfilling eight wishes, the fish b had to wait about thirty years for the ninth; the sheik was very old by this point and couldn't remember his last wish. The fish gained much weight and stopped weeping. They probably got used to their new life.

'Bruno and Buba established a repair workshop for vacuum cleaners in Hamburg.

'I personally didn't know the crows too well, as after that unfortunate business trip with Ben they rarely visited our house. Each time they came, they tried to involve Ben in some strange deal. They intensified their pressure on Ben when they heard about the treasure found by the horse. But when Ben categorically told them that he was not interested in their ideas, they stopped coming to us. Someone told me that one of their ideas worked out, and they made a fortune. They bought a Greek island and spent their days on the beach being burned by sun and cigars and wiled away their evenings playing cards.

'Rudelfin married Rudolfo Violentino, who was a scientist. Her family at first didn't want to allow her to marry Rudolfo because of the grey colour of his fur, but Rudelfin's and Rudolf's love was so strong that eventually that opposition to their marriage crumbled. A couple of years after their wedding, Rudolfo took with him his wife for a science trip to the Brazilian jungle. That was about forty years ago. Since then, they have vanished. Several international rescue teams went to the jungle to search for them, but in vain. However, I heard on the television news that a year ago a herd of strange two-coloured squirrels, that is, red and grey, were discovered in the Brazilian jungle.

'From all those animals, only Bertha was left in the house with us. She died of age.

'Ross signed a contract with a studio in Tokyo and performed in the television series *The Three Musketeers*. And when he could no longer play a musketeer because of his weight, he settled in the Italian Alps where he married and had lots of children. The last I heard, he was giving sumo lessons.

'The Great Bear Tysh and Chopinowicz organized and played classical music on modern instruments. Tysh on the peak of his career was so famous that the whole world listened to his songs.

'He died tragically with his entire group in an aeroplane crash. The whole world mourned him for many years – until the appearance of Elvis Presley.

'Albert, as could be expected, got a butler job at Buckingham Palace. He didn't want to leave us, as he was very loyal, but when the Queen came personally and begged him to go to London, he left for England, together with Kikiru and their countless breed.'

'That's all I can remember, and I am probably the last witness of those happenings.'

It was now very late, well after midnight, and the youngest of the listeners were lying in inert poses, sleeping hard. All of the others were sitting motionless, as if still listening to the last words that Grannie had said. Nikki got up and, unnoticed by anyone, went to the portrait of Grandpa Ben and asked, 'Is it true, Granddaddy?'

Grandfather smiled back mysteriously. He neither denied nor confirmed.

## About the Author and Illustrator

**Agatha Jane** was born in Johannesburg. She lived her adolescence years in Belgium and her adult life in Poland. At present she lives in London.

She wrote this book at the age of eighteen. She studied film directing and script writing at the Camerimage Film School in Toruń. Being passionate about comedies, she gets to disguise herself as known and less-known people to make others laugh. She loves travelling and is an accomplished mother (she's expecting her second child) and is a cheerful woman.

**Victoira Jankiewicz-Pezler** has a master's degree in political sciences. She is married and is the mother of two children.

She left the fuss of city life for the peaceful countryside. She likes to fish (which are immediately released back into the water), and she likes mushrooming (each single piece is checked thoroughly, and unwelcome inhabitants must leave the mushroom). Anthony and the Johnsons is her favourite band.

CPSIA information can be obtained
at www.ICGtesting.com
Printed in the USA
LVIC040932201212
3248LVUK00002BA

* 9 7 8 1 4 7 7 2 4 6 9 3 1 *